MY FATHER IS
IN THE NAVY

by Robin McKinley
pictures by
Martine Gourbault

Greenwillow Books, New York

Colored pencils were used for the full-color art.
The text type is Cochin.

Text copyright © 1992 by Robin McKinley
Illustrations copyright © 1992 by Martine Gourbault
All rights reserved. No part of this book may be reproduced
or utilized in any form or by any means, electronic or mechanical,
including photocopying, recording, or by any information storage
and retrieval system, without permission in writing from the Publisher,
Greenwillow Books, a division of William Morrow & Company, Inc.,
1350 Avenue of the Americas, New York, NY 10019.
Printed in Hong Kong by South China Printing Company (1988) Ltd.
First Edition   10 9 8 7 6 5 4 3 2 1

Library of Congress Cataloging-in-Publication Data
McKinley, Robin.
    My father is in the Navy / by Robin McKinley ;
pictures by Martine Gourbault.
        p.   cm.
        Summary: A young girl doesn't remember her father,
a ship's captain who has been at sea.
        ISBN 0-688-10639-0. ISBN 0-688-10640-4 (lib. bdg.)
        [1. Fathers — Fiction.]   I. Gourbault, Martine, ill.
II. Title.   PZ7.M1988My   1992
[E]—dc20   91-12566   CIP   AC

TO GEORGE
— R. McK.

TO GILLEAN
— M. G.

My mother and I lived in
a little house with a big yard

and a kitten named Ernest.

Every night when my mother put me to bed, she read me a story. After the story one night she said, "Guess what? Daddy's coming home. He'll be home on Saturday. He'll be so glad to see you! You've grown so much. It's been a long time."

Then she kissed me and turned out the light. Ernest stalked up my leg, purring, and curled up in his place under my chin. I hugged him.

I didn't remember my father.

My mother talked about him a lot.
She read me the letters my father
wrote us.
But I didn't remember him.
Most of my friends had
fathers who lived with them.
Sometimes their fathers lived
somewhere else, and my friends
visited them. I knew to say,
"My daddy is in the Navy,"
when anyone asked me about
my father.

But I didn't remember him.

There was a picture of him on
the mantel in the living room.
I knew to say, "Good night, Daddy,"
when I went to bed.

But I didn't remember him.
I didn't tell my mother.

She was excited.
On Saturday we put on
our best dresses.

Ernest sat in the window
as we left.

It was a long drive to the place
where the ship was coming in.
There were a lot of people there
already. They were all excited, too.

I didn't feel excited.

"What's the matter with you?"
my mother said. "These are all
the other families whose daddies
are on your daddy's ship."
She said hello to a lot of
the other mothers.

I didn't say hello to anyone.

"We are up front because your daddy's the captain,"
my mother said. "The ship's almost here."
My mother picked me up so I could see better.

The ship was big and gray — bigger than our house,
and much taller. It slid slowly toward us through
the water. There were lots of people waving.

Men on the dock held up
their hands for the huge
loops of rope the men on
the ship threw down to them.
"There he is!" said my
mother. Her voice was
very high and happy.
"Look! Over there!"
She was waving.

I didn't see anybody I knew.

The gangplank came down, and
people started hurrying off the ship.
My mother rushed forward.
I hid my face in her neck.
"Well, aren't you going to say hello
to me, Sara?" said a deep voice.

I looked up.

And then I remembered my father.